Polar Bolero
Debi Gliori

Hippo

For Jo, my mum, with all my love.

Scholastic Children's Books,
Commonwealth House, 1~19 New Oxford Street,
London WC1A 1NU, UK
a division of Scholastic Ltd
London ~ New York ~ Toronto ~ Sydney ~ Auckland
Mexico City ~ New Delhi ~ Hong Kong

First published by David Fickling Books, an imprint of Scholastic Ltd, 2000
This paperback edition published by Scholastic, 2001

Text and illustrations copyright   Debi Gliori, 2000

ISBN: 0 439 01372 0 Hardback
ISBN: 0 439 99266 4 Paperback

Printed in Belgium.
All rights reserved

2 4 6 8 10 9 7 5 3 1

The story's beginning . . .

. . . and the moon's
flying high

trailing fat clouds
across the night sky

. . . and creep . . .

I'm a thing

that goes BUMP

in the night.

out the door

past the gate

through the deep summer grasses to the edge of the lawn, with the things that are LUMPS in the night.

And here is the hill
where the
wide~awake meet

in peejays and slippers and some with bare feet.

There is music and laughter
drifting up from the trees

as we Polar Bolero with the owls and the bees

over oceans
and mountains
across rivers
and streams

the Polar Bolero makes
you JUMP in your dreams.

So . . . we're flying back home to where somebody cares, falling into our pillows, tightly hugging our bears.

In the dark comes
that someone
who goes HUG
in the night

kisses me gently

and whispers, "Goodnight."